MIDNIGHT

EMPIRE

NASHA PERRY

Midnight Empire
Copyright © 2026 by Nasha Perry

ISBN: 979-8-9987951-4-5

Printed in the USA by A'Lure Publishing, LLC (alurepublishing.net)

DEDICATION

To my mother.
You built me solid.
You built me sharp.
You built me unstoppable.
Everything I conquer is rooted in you.

TABLE OF CONTENTS

INTRODUCTION

They say every queen remembers the moment she stopped being a girl.

Mine didn't happen in a ballroom.

It didn't come with a crown.

It came with hunger.

Not the kind that growls in your stomach—the kind that whispers in your spirit when you realize love doesn't pay bills... and loyalty doesn't guarantee survival.

I wasn't born cold.

I was born soft.

Country-raised. Church on Sundays. Dirt roads and front porch secrets. I believed in forever. I believed in first love. I believed that if you were good enough, the world would be kind back.

I was wrong.

The city didn't care about my innocence.

Men didn't care about my dreams.

And the world doesn't reward girls who wait to be chosen.

So I stopped waiting.

What started as survival became strategy.

What started as heartbreak became leverage.

And what started as a secret... became an empire.

They'll call me manipulative.

They'll call me dangerous.

They'll call me everything but what I really am.

Self-made.

But before the headlines, before the Velvet Circle, before the name that makes powerful men lower their voices…

There was just me.

Savannah.

And the night I realized if I wanted control…

I would have to take it.

This is not a love story.

This is the story of how I learned the difference between love and power—and why I chose power.

Vanna

She Is Escaping to Become Everything.

CHAPTER ONE

GOODBYE DIRT ROADS

The dirt crunched under Savannah's boots as she stepped off the porch for the last time. The sun had barely started to rise, casting soft gold over the rusted fields and half-dead cotton rows that lined her daddy's broken-down land. She didn't look back. There was nothing worth remembering—just ghosts, pain, and dreams that never made it past the county line.

At eighteen, Savannah Mae Tucker had already lived a thousand hard days. Her mama had died when she was fifteen, breast cancer coming fast and cruel. Her daddy had drowned his grief in Jack Daniel's and spit it back out in slurred curses and swinging fists. This place was a cage wrapped in barbed-wire memories, and she was done.

The Greyhound bus moaned as it pulled up, kicking up dust like it was trying to erase her footsteps. She slung her thrift-store duffel over her shoulder, took a breath thick with diesel and goodbye, and climbed on. One-way ticket to Atlanta. One hundred and thirty-four dollars in her pocket. No plans. No friends. Just a fire in her chest and a voice in her head whispering: *You ain't meant to die in a place like this.*

The ride was long. Farm roads turned to highways. Barns gave way to billboards. By the time the skyline broke through the horizon, all steel and glitter, her heart was thudding with a mix of fear and thrill.

She stepped off that bus like a fawn in the jungle—wide-eyed, hopeful, and completely unaware of the wolves waiting in the dark.

CHAPTER TWO

FIRST TASTE OF THE CITY

The air smelled different here—like exhaust, ambition, and fast money. Atlanta didn't whisper like the country. It roared. Big wheels squealed down Peachtree. Neon signs buzzed like they were high on their own light. Everything moved fast—cars, people, even time.

Savannah stepped onto the cracked pavement in a sundress and cowboy boots, standing out like a hymnal at a strip club. She clutched her bag tighter, scanning unfamiliar streets. Her phone was nearly dead. No service. No plan. But she kept walking.

The bus station was downtown—loud, dirty, and full of stories no one told. She found a corner store, spent her last five dollars on a charger and a bag of chips, and sat on the curb while her phone came back to life.

That's when she appeared.

Tall. Chocolate-skinned. Braids down to her waist. Thigh-high red boots.

A black romper that hugged every curve. A smirk like she owned the street.

"You lost, lil' country?" the girl asked.

Savannah hesitated. "Just . . . new here."

The girl laughed. "No shit. You look like you came off the rodeo float."

Savannah should've been offended. But there was no venom—just truth.

"I'm Jazmine," she said, extending a manicured hand that sparkled like diamonds. "And lucky for you, I know how to survive this city. You hungry?"

Savannah nodded before her stomach could growl.

An hour later, they were at a tiny diner tucked between a pawnshop and a hookah lounge. Savannah devoured a cheeseburger while Jazmine watched with amused curiosity.

"So, what's your story?" Jazmine asked.

Savannah wiped her mouth. "Grew up in the sticks. Mama's dead; Daddy's useless. I'm just tryna make it."

Jazmine tilted her head, eyes narrowing. "You pretty— soft face, big eyes, them curves. You could get paid."

Savannah frowned. "Paid to do what?"

Jazmine leaned in close, voice low and sultry. "To be wanted. To be desired. To make a man forget his wife, his bills, his problems. You ever heard of high-end escorting?"

Savannah blinked.

Jazmine sat back, smirking. "You got that 'new girl' glow. Men eat that up.

I could show you the ropes. You'd make more in one night than a waitress does in two weeks."

Savannah looked down at her empty plate. Her stomach was full, but her head spun. Was this what her mama would want? Maybe not. But her mama wasn't here. And the rent in Atlanta didn't care about morals.

"I ain't no ho," she whispered.

Jazmine laughed. "Baby girl, this ain't the blade. This is luxury. Class. You pick the clients, you set the rules. Ain't no pimps here—only bosses. You wanna cry broke or you wanna boss up?"

Savannah didn't answer. Not yet. But in that moment, she knew one thing for sure: The country was gone, and the city was calling.

CHAPTER THREE

LACED IN LACE

The apartment Jazmine took Savannah to was nothing like she expected. Marble floors. Velvet couches. Mirrors on every wall. The whole place smelled like vanilla and ambition.

"This ain't where I live," Jazmine said, tossing her keys onto the counter. "This is where I work."

Savannah's eyes followed her reflection from wall to wall. Every surface showed her differently: softer here, sharper there. Jazmine poured two glasses of Moscato and handed one to her.

"You run all this?" Savannah asked.

Jazmine smirked. "I run me. That's all that matters."

She nodded toward the back room. "Time to find your look."

Inside, Savannah stood barefoot while Jazmine held up outfit after outfit—lace bodysuits, thigh-high stockings, silky robes. Finally, they landed on a rose-gold lingerie set that hugged her curves like it had been stitched for her soul.

"You look like money," Jazmine said, lighting a blunt. "But you gotta move like it too."

Savannah swallowed. "What if I mess up?"

"First rule?" Jazmine exhaled slowly. "Don't fake it. Walk in like you belong. If you believe it, they will too."

That night Savannah had her first booking.

His name was Derrick. Mid-thirties. Clean-cut. Corporate. A lawyer with a thing for southern accents. He'd paid double for a new face.

In the back of the Uber, Savannah's hands trembled. Her mama's voice flickered faintly in her head—then faded like an old gospel record skipping in the wind.

The hotel was five-star. Chandeliers. Marble floors. Doormen in tuxedos. Her heels clicked like gunshots on tile.

Derrick was waiting in the penthouse for Savannah. He had a gentle smile. No pressure. No rush. Just conversation, wine, and curiosity.

"You from Mississippi?" he asked.

"Alabama," she said, her voice soft with a southern twang. "Country born and bred."

He smiled. "That's sexy."

It didn't go how she imagined. No cheap moves. No shame. Just discovery—how to control a room with eye contact, laughter, silence.

When it was over, he left $2,000 on the nightstand.

Two. Thousand. Dollars. More than her daddy made in a month fixing engines and broken promises.

In the Uber home, Savannah stared at her reflection— lipstick smeared, hair wild, cheeks flushed.

She didn't feel dirty.

She felt powerful.

A part of her had awakened. The country girl was still there, but now she wore lace and played by new rules.

Her phone buzzed with a text from Jazmine.

How was it?

Savannah typed one word.

Addictive.

Jazmine

Nurturing, Street Smart, and Quietly Surviving the Game

CHAPTER FOUR

THE REBRAND

In the days after that first night, something inside Savannah shifted. A quiet, resilient girl who once wore faded denim and scuffed boots was shedding skin. There was no going back. She was destined to be reborn, not just as an escort but as a force to be reckoned with.

Savannah spent hours poring over her reflection in mismatched mirrors at Jazmine's apartment.

Every morning felt like a rehearsal.

The shadows on her face—the deep lines of pain, the whispers of regret—were slowly replaced by an emerging spark of self-assurance. She began to study the women who ruled these glittering city streets and learned how they carried themselves, the way they dressed, even how they spoke in soft yet commanding tones.

Jazmine studied her like an artist. "Baby, you got spark," she said. "Let's give it a name."

She laid out clothes—a sleek blazer paired with a satin blouse, a high-waisted pencil skirt, and accessories that shined as if they were made from a captured dream. "How about *Vanna*," Jazmine said. "Means *renewal*. That's what you are—a rebirth."

Savannah hesitated at first. *Vanna* sounded like someone else's story—a persona set apart from the girl who had left the country with nothing but hope and tenacious will to change. But as she tried on the clothes, something unexpected happened. With every adjustment of her hair, every carefully applied stroke of lipstick, she felt her old self melt away. In her reflection the raw, vulnerable girl was replaced by a confident, enigmatic woman whose eyes burned with determination.

Standing before the mirror fully transformed, she whispered her new name. "I am Vanna now." The words felt like both a promise and a challenge—a declaration to the world that she was ready to harness her potential and master the game. Gone was the image of a lost country girl; instead, there stood a woman armed with elegance and grit, poised to conquer every room she entered.

The transformation wasn't just skin deep. Vanna began to rewrite the rules of her existence. With Jazmine's guidance, she learned how to curate her image not as an object of desire but as a symbol of empowerment. In carefully crafted social media posts, in the confident, measured tone she used with everyone around her, Vanna slowly reclaimed her narrative.

Every garment, every accessory, became a tool in her arsenal—a means to forge a new identity from the scars of her past. She began to think like a strategist: If she was going to succeed in the high-stakes world of luxury escorting, she'd need to move beyond the simple exchange of desire for cash. It was time to captivate minds and hearts, to be more than a pretty face; she was now a brand.

In the quiet moments between appointments, Vanna took long walks along the neon-lit streets of Alanta, pondering her future. She saw the city as a living, breathing entity—its chaos and beauty reflecting her own inner turmoil and aspirations. Each step was both liberation and rebirth. The transformation was not just about adopting a new name or style; it was about claiming power over her own narrative, turning vulnerability into strength.

By the end of the week, Vanna wasn't just recognized as the fresh face in a bustling industry. She became known for something deeper, a presence that commanded respect, a mystery that drew people in. The country girl was a part of her past, but *Vanna* was her future. And that future was hers to shape, one carefully chosen encounter at a time.

Kia Loyal

CHAPTER FIVE

HUSTLER'S HEART

Vanna learned fast: Beauty opened doors, but hustle kept them open.

Every night blurred into the next.

Black cars. Rooftop suites. Expensive dinners with men who smelled like money and secrets. She wasn't just getting booked—she was getting *chosen*. Word was spreading. A southern girl with a soft drawl, killer curves, and a gaze that could melt steel? Vanna was in demand. She moved like she'd been born for this. Classy, discreet, always in control. Clients respected her. Some even adored her. Jazmine started joking, "You gon' be the next madam if you keep running through my regulars."

But beneath the champagne and Chanel was a grind that never slept.

Vanna kept a burner phone, tracked every dollar, every booking. She turned her body into a business. Her lips into a brand. She paid attention—watched how Jazmine negotiated, how the other girls moved, and where they slipped up. She knew looks would only get her so far.

One night she met Kia, a wild, fire-tongued girl from New Orleans who dressed like a vixen and had zero filter.

"Girl, you movin' too quiet," Kia said, filing her nails. "You makin' all that money, somebody gon' notice."

Vanna didn't flinch. "Let 'em."

Kia raised a brow. "Confidence is cute. But watch your back. These streets don't play fair." It wasn't long before Vanna learned that lesson firsthand.

One Friday night, after a high-end booking in Buckhead, she returned to her Airbnb to find the place trashed. Her bags dumped. Her stash—gone. Five grand. Jewelry. Lingerie. Even her burner phone. No forced entry. No signs of a break-in. Which meant it had been someone on the inside. Her mind went straight to Toya—a girl she'd been friendly with, once shared rides with. Lately Toya had been giving her side-eyes and cold smiles. Vanna had out-booked her three weekends in a row.

Jazmine confirmed it. "Toya's mad you passin' her. This game got no sisters, just survivors."

Vanna didn't cry. She didn't scream.

She watched. She learned.

Then she got even.

Within a week she had switched up her location, changed all her contacts, and started screening clients tighter. No more casual convos with the girls she didn't trust. She booked directly, negotiated harder, and made sure everyone knew—Vanna wasn't one to play.

And her stolen money? She tripled it back within days. Because men weren't paying for sex. They were paying for Vanna—an experience, a fantasy, a secret they'd beg to keep.

But even as her pockets swelled and her name started buzzing in the right circles, she could feel the danger breathing down her neck. Atlanta was sweet at the surface—but deep down it had fangs. And the more she climbed, the more snakes slithered close. Vanna sat on her balcony once scared. Not anymore. She understood now that this wasn't just about money. This was about power. And she was coming for all of it.

CHAPTER SIX

BOSS UP OR BOW OUT

The moment Vanna decided to go solo, everything shifted. No more splitting cuts with Jazmine. No more depending on bookings that came through someone's phone. If she was going to risk it all, she was going to own it all. It started with a notebook. A cheap one from the gas station. In it she wrote down her vision: No pimps. No drama. No low ballers. Just high-end clients, high-dollar rates, and women who looked like walking wealth.

She named it the Velvet Circle.

The branding came next: photoshoots in luxury hotel rooms, silk sheets, wine glasses, soft lighting. She hired a discreet photographer who specialized in lifestyle branding for exotic dancers and models. Classy, not raunchy. Power in every pose. Vanna was always front and center—her face partially hidden, her aura unmistakable.

Then the roster. Girls she trusted. Not many—just three.

Kia, the wild one with a jaw-dropping body and a hustler's hustle.

Brielle, soft-spoken and caramel toned, looked like she belonged in a '90s R&B music video.

Naomi, part-time bottle girl, full-time savage—light eyes, darker secrets.

Vanna didn't just book them; she trained them. Taught them how to move, how to talk, how to set boundaries without breaking the fantasy.

She built a code: Luxury only. Respect always.

No finessing the clients—but no selling yourself cheap either.

Word spread quickly. The Velvet Circle was different. No drama. No mess. Just premium companionship for men who could afford the silence that came with beauty. By the end of the first month, Vanna was clearing $30K. By month two, she was booking international trips—Dubai, London, Turks and Caicos.

The money was beautiful. But the power was addictive.

Men who used to control her time were now requesting her schedule. Clients who once talked slick now addressed her like royalty. And the girls? They looked at her like a queen pin. Someone who'd cracked the code and pulled them up with her.

But with power came problems. Old heads in the city started whispering. Jazmine kept her distance but sent a warning text: You movin' fast, ma. Careful who you outshine.

Vanna wasn't worried about shadows. She was too focused on the spotlight. She bought a loft in Midtown. All glass and gold, overlooking the city she was conquering. She redecorated it in velvet, marble, and custom art—everything about it screamed arrival.

One night while smoking hookah with Kia and Brielle, she said it out loud for the first time.

"I ain't just in the game no more. I am the game." They clinked glasses, toasting to bad bitches and bigger bags.

But deep in her chest, Vanna felt it—something stirring. A sense that the higher you climbed, the thinner the air got. And somewhere out there, someone was watching. Waiting. Plotting.

But she didn't flinch. Not even a blink.

Because Vanna wasn't backing down.

She was just getting started.

Brielle

Once Loyal, Now Walking the Line...

CHAPTER SEVEN

ENEMIES IN DESIGNER

The warning came through a DM.

Watch ya circle. Not everybody praying for you.

No name, no profile pic. Just a message that hit different. Vanna ignored it at first. She had bigger things to focus on—two out-of-town bookings, an exclusive client flying in from London, and Brielle prepping for her first solo trip to Miami. Business was booming, and the Velvet Circle was finally operating like a well-oiled luxury machine.

But the second warning couldn't be ignored. A client canceled at the last minute—her client. A regular. High-paying. Loyal. When she followed up, his message was short and cold: *Heard some things gotta step back.*

She felt it in her chest—tight, sharp.

Something wasn't right.

She started digging. Turned out, someone was spreading rumors that the Velvet Circle was sloppy. That Vanna wasn't managing the girls—she was pimping them. That she was pocketing extra from bookings. Clients were being told not to trust her.

The source?

Toya.

The same girl who had set her up months ago, back when Vanna was still learning how to walk in heels on Atlanta's sharp streets. But Toya wasn't just salty anymore—she was strategic. She had linked up with another escort ring, run by a shady ex-stripper named Lexxi, who was known for burning girls and ghosting clients with deposits. They were trying to paint Vanna as a fraud. A scammer. A middleman pretending to be elite. Vanna knew what it was: envy dressed in Fendi. But she couldn't just respond with tweets and subliminal messages. She needed a move that said Queen, not rookie. So she played it smart.

She hosted a private event—The Velvet Soiree. Invitation-only. Black-tie. Exclusive venue. A-list clientele. She hired security, rented out a penthouse lounge, and styled every girl in floor-length gowns, diamonds, and poise. No sex. No bookings. Just luxury. Just presence. The message was loud and clear:

This ain't the street. This is a brand.

The event was a hit. Clients whispered about the class. Other girls begged to join. Sponsors started reaching out. Blogs picked it up. Even local influencers reposted.

Toya and Lexxi? Silent. But that didn't mean they were done.

Vanna sat in her Bentley that night, watching Atlanta flicker beneath her. Her phone buzzed. It was Kia.

"Yo I heard Lexxi talking reckless at Gold Room. She said you ain't built for this long-term."

Vanna smirked.

"Let her talk. I'm building an empire while she's chasing deposits." But deep down, she knew this wasn't over. Toya was petty. Lexxi was ruthless. And in this business, envy didn't shoot warning shots.

CHAPTER EIGHT

PAST AIN'T DEAD

It started with a knock. Not the kind that came with room service or a client arriving early. No, this knock was heavy. Familiar. Like it came with dirt on its boots. Vanna had just lit a candle in her loft, silk robe tied loose, face bare. She wasn't expecting anyone. When she opened the door, her world froze.

"Hey, Sav."

Nobody in Atlanta called her that.

It was *Deon.*

Her ex. The only boy she'd ever loved back in that dusty little town with one gas station and too many broken dreams. The one who had promised he'd marry her, then disappeared when her mama got sick and her life fell apart. He looked the same but older. A few tattoos now. Scruff on his jaw. Eyes that still knew too much.

"What the hell are you doing here?" Vanna asked, stepping into the doorway like a shield.

He scratched his neck, nervous. "I been lookin' for you, girl. For a while. Saw you on somebody's Snapchat story. Real fancy now, huh?"

Vanna's heart was thumping, but her face stayed calm.

"You came all this way . . . for a Snapchat?"

"Nah," he said, looking down at his beat-up sneakers. "I came 'cause I miss you. 'Cause I ain't stopped thinking 'bout you since you left."

She scoffed. "You didn't think about me when I was sleeping in my car. Or when Mama died. Or when I was breaking my back just to eat noodles and keep gas in the tank." He looked ashamed.

Good.

"I messed up," he said. "But I'm here now. And I can tell you got real people around you that don't *know* you. Not like I do." That line hit too close. Because he was right.

Nobody in Atlanta knew Savannah. The real her. The girl who used to sing in the church, wore sundresses in the summer, cried when her dog had died. Vanna had buried that girl—but now she was being dragged back up, breath by breath.

"I got my own life now," she said, folding her arms. "And you're not a part of it."

But Deon didn't leave. He stayed in Atlanta. Started popping up. Once at a bar where she was meeting a client. Another time outside her gym. Just standing there.

Kia noticed. "You know that dude been circling your block twice a week? You need to handle that." Vanna felt the walls closing in. Her two worlds couldn't mix. If clients started connecting dots, everything could fall apart. Deon didn't know the game. He didn't understand discretion. He was too raw, too country, and too *loud.* Worse—he still had a piece of her heart.

CHAPTER NINE

THE FALL OR THE FLEX

It was a ping.

Then another.

Then her phone lit up like a slot machine on fire.

Text after text. Missed calls. DMs with cryptic messages like:

You good?

This you, V?

Damn . . . they really tried you.

She clicked the first link a client had sent.

And there it was.

A photo.

Grainy. Snapped through a hotel room window. But still clear enough to see her: bent over, half-naked, a client behind her. His face blurred—but hers? Unmistakable. Vanna's throat dried. She dropped the phone. She couldn't breathe. This wasn't just some random leak. It was an attack. Somebody wanted her gone.

She went into full lockdown. Pulled the girls in. Had Kia sweep through socials, had Naomi clear the booking calendar. Shut the website down. Disappeared from IG. Became silent. But the city wasn't quiet.

The blogs picked it up.

"Luxury Escort Queen Exposed?"

"The Velvet Circle Caught Slipping."

Clients backed out. A lawyer client she trusted ghosted her. Sponsors? Silent. Money stopped moving. Fast.

She knew exactly who it was: Lexxi.

Only someone that pressed and messy would risk exposing herself just to smear Vanna's name. But she didn't have proof yet. And in the game of power, emotion was a liability.

She sat in her loft, looking out over the city, back against the cold window. For the first time in months, she felt small. Vulnerable. "Was it all for nothing?" she whispered to herself. But then she caught sight of her reflection in the glass.

Not Savannah.

Not scared.

Vanna.

And Vanna didn't fold.

She flipped her phone on, went live on her private platform—the one her elite clients subscribed to. No music. No filter. Just her. Wrapped in silk, face bare, voice low.

"I know y'all seen it," she said. "So let's be clear. I am who I say I am. I don't owe nobody shame. I owe myself power. You want scandal? Make sure you mention how I turned pain into profit. How I fed women who had nothing. How I turned a name into a brand. And if you still wanna judge me . . . then just make sure you spell my name right."

The video went viral.

Clients—real ones—started texting again. One text read: *That wasn't a fall. That was a flex. You more real than all these chicks frontin'.*

By the end of the week, bookings started to bounce back. Not all. But enough. She even got a call from a woman in L.A.—wanted to collab. Build a sister circle out west.

Expansion.

Vanna lit a blunt, exhaled slowly. They tried to break her. They handed her a scandal, and she turned it into a statement. Because real queens don't run from war. They turn every bullet into a badge.

Nova New To The City

But Ready To Take Over

CHAPTER TEN

EMPIRE STATE OF MIND

Atlanta was just the beginning.

After the scandal, after the silence, after the smoke cleared—Vanna didn't just bounce back. She rebranded.

She wasn't just an escort anymore. She was a mogul.

The Velvet Circle wasn't just a name—it was a movement. A discreet, curated, and powerful luxury lifestyle network where sex was only the surface. The real currency was access, experience, and control. And now, it was time to expand.

Vanna touched down in New York like she owned the skyline. Long mink. Black shades. Designer heels clicking on the JFK floors like she was walking on gold. Brielle was already there, setting up the new base—an upscale penthouse in SoHo, all-white everything, marble countertops, and floor-to-ceiling windows.

The Velvet Circle NYC was lean, just two handpicked girls from Atlanta and one new recruit: Nova, a fashion student with a slick mouth and a walk that turned heads in every borough.

The clientele?

Different. Richer. Colder.

They didn't care about the soft southern charm—these men wanted exclusivity. Mystery.

Sophistication with bite. And Vanna gave them exactly that.

She started throwing hush-hush invite only events in art galleries, partnering with Black-owned luxury brands, hosting "socialite mixers" that doubled as clients vetting spots. She wasn't selling sex—she was selling a fantasy lifestyle with rules.

One night she stood on a rooftop overlooking Manhattan, wind in her hair, Nova beside her. "You really built this outta nothing," Nova said, sipping her champagne. Vanna smiled. "I built it outta pain. That's a different kind of foundation."

Back in Atlanta, Kia was holding it down. In Miami, Brielle was scouting locations. In L.A., she had a meeting with a talent agent who wanted to rebrand escorts as luxury muses for film execs and pro athletes.

This was bigger than bookings now.

It was business. Branding. Influence.

She wasn't in rooms anymore—she was owning them.

But she never forgot the cost.

There were still threats. Still whispers. Deon was still in the city, quiet, watching.

Lexxi had gone dark—too dark. And Vanna knew the deeper you moved in shadows, the closer you got to danger. But she was ready. Because she wasn't some pretty face trying to survive.

She was a CEO. And every step she took was legacy in motion.

CHAPTER ELEVEN

LEGEND STATUS

Vanna always knew the game had an expiration date. Not the money. Not the fame. The peace. And tonight, it was all cracking at once. She got the call at 2:14 a.m.

"It's Kia. Somebody snatched her."

The voice on the phone was Nova's. Shaking. Out of breath.

Kia had been out in Atlanta meeting a new client, a referral from a client Vanna used to trust. But it was a setup. No trace. Just a broken heel in a hotel stairwell and a burner phone tossed in the trash. Vanna froze for one second. Then the beast inside her woke up. She jumped on the first flight back to ATL, her mind spinning the whole ride.

This wasn't random.

This wasn't street-level drama. This was a hit. Someone was trying to take her out by targeting her circle. And she had a pretty damn good idea who was behind it.

Lexxi.

The bitter queen with a bruised ego. The one who had disappeared after Vanna took over the scene. But now, she'd resurfaced—louder, dirtier, and more reckless than ever. Word on the street was that Lexxi had partnered with a dirty promoter and was trying to build her own "elite" roster by poaching Vanna's girls.

By force.

Vanna knew she had to move smart. Not emotional. So she called in favors. Pulled from her highest-tier clients— lawyers, a private investigator, even a retired cop she once turned down. Within forty-eight hours, they had found Kia. Tied up but alive. Shaken and bruised but not broken.

Vanna stayed silent the whole ride to the loft. But when they walked in, and Kia finally broke down crying, something in Vanna snapped. She knew what she had to do.

No more branding. No more press kits. War.

She pulled up to Lexxi's little "networking party" uninvited—heels clicking like gunshots, black leather on, ice in her stare. The room went still when she walked in. Vanna didn't say a word at first. Just stood there. Let her presence speak. Then she locked eyes with Lexxi and said, "You got one more time to touch mine. After that? I'm not just ruining your name. I'm ending your entire legacy."

Lexxi smirked, but her hands were shaking. Because everyone in the room saw it now. Vanna wasn't just that girl. She was the girl. The room parted for her as she left. Like a queen in a battlefield of pawns.

Later that night Vanna sat on her rooftop, smoking slow. Watching the skyline like it was a map she had conquered. The girls were safe. The business was booming. New chapters were forming in Vegas and Houston. Even whispers about a Velvet

Circle documentary were floating around. She was no longer surviving. She was documented history.

A country girl from nothing who turned scandal into strategy. Pain into power. And the game?

She didn't just play it.

She redefined it.

PREVIEW

Book 2: Black Swan

CHAPTER ONE

THE GIRL IN PARIS

The body wasn't supposed to be discovered until morning.

By then, the client would've been gone. The sheets replaced. The penthouse scrubbed clean. But someone wanted her found. They wanted the blood visible. The panic immediate. The message delivered.

Pinned to her wrist with a diamond-studded safety pin was a single black feather. And across the mirror, written in red: *VELVET BLEEDS.*

In New York, Vanna's phone began to ring.

She didn't know it yet, but the empire she'd built was already under attack.